A Clearing in the Forest

A Story About A Real Settler Boy

JOANNE LANDERS HENRY

ILLUSTRATED BY CHARLES ROBINSON

FOUR WINDS PRESS ❖ NEW YORK

MAXWELL MACMILLAN CANADA *Toronto*

MAXWELL MACMILLAN INTERNATIONAL

New York   Oxford   Singapore   Sydney

The author wishes to thank her mother, Octavia Greene Landers, former teacher and native Hoosier, for help with the research; the Indiana Historical Society, for permission to use materials from an unpublished manuscript by Elijah Fletcher and from *The Diary of Calvin Fletcher*, vol. I, published by the society in 1972; the historian's office of Conner Prairie, an outdoor history museum near Indianapolis, for contributing to the research; and the librarians of the Indianapolis–Marion County Public Library, the Indiana State Library, and the William Henry Smith Memorial Library of the Indiana Historical Society for their assistance.

To my parents,
Octavia Greene Landers and Delver Landers,
native Hoosiers of another generation

—J.L.H.

ONE

El's Choice

"Yeah, yeah, broken-nose Yankee!" shouted Amos, one of the biggest boys in Elijah Fletcher's school. He bumped against El on purpose as he charged out the schoolroom door.

"That's what you get for always having your nose stuck up in the air, El Fletcher," another boy added with a smirk.

El could feel his face turn hot with anger. He wished he were big and tall enough to fight back.

His nose throbbed with pain, and the knuckles of his right hand were swollen. Schoolmaster Gregg had struck hard with the ferule, a ruler he used to punish scholars.

Nine-year-old El waited while the bigger boys pushed and shoved their way out of the school. At last he made his way outside into the gray, chilly November air. He looked around for his older brother, Cooley, who had been one of the first out the door. Then he caught sight of Cooley racing south on Delaware Street—clearly not headed home.

Despite his pain, El decided to follow Cooley and see where he was going. He scurried after his brother, hoping he could catch up. Ten-year-old Cooley's long, skinny legs gave him an advantage over El's much shorter, stockier ones. He could always beat El in a race.

El's round face was still hot with anger at Schoolmaster Gregg's cruelty and the taunts of Amos and his friend. Amos was just a slow-moving, slow-talking country boy. He and his folks had come from down South.

El was proud that his father came from back East—Vermont—and his mother from Ohio. Many of the town's settlers—craftsmen, businessmen, doctors, and lawyers—had come from the East. They had brought with them their Yankee ways, which some of the southern country folks didn't like.

Still trying to keep up with Cooley, who had turned onto Washington

Street, El skirted a few half-rotted tree stumps scattered along its edge. Washington Street was part of the much-talked-about National Road, which was being built from Cumberland, Maryland, to the western frontier.

Now, in 1833, the wide section of the road that ran through Indianapolis was paved with broken stone and gravel. Many of the other streets in Indianapolis were not paved. They were ridged and rutty where wagon wheels had pressed into the soft earth, which dried unevenly and as hard as stone. When it rained, wagons sank into the mud up to their axles, and buggies got mired down.

El hurried on. Impatiently he dodged around a fast-moving buggy, several riders on horseback, and a heavy Conestoga freight wagon pulled by three teams of horses. Drivers and riders would not take kindly to a boy getting in their way or frightening their horses.

He could remember Father's stern voice warning him to pay heed to the traffic. Just last week a runaway horse had dragged a buggy onto the wood-plank walk in front of the *Indiana Journal* newspaper office. The driver had been badly hurt, almost killed.

Ahead El could still see Cooley. He was well past the brick building where Father's law office was. Nearby was the frame two-story Washington Hall Hotel, which dwarfed the small bank building nearby.

Suddenly Cooley ducked behind a bright blue freight wagon and disappeared from sight.

Sighing, El slowed to a walk. It seemed as if he was always trying to keep up with Cooley, even with Cooley's dreams of adventure.

Cooley said that when he grew up, he was going to leave Indianapolis. After all, he said, it was just an ordinary small town in a clearing in the forest. Some folks called it a hog hole. Cooley dreamed of going back East or maybe even to some foreign country. He might become a famous artist someday, he bragged.

Father, who was a lawyer, didn't put much store in Cooley's boasts. He said being an artist was no way to earn a living. He didn't put much store in what the naysayers had to say about Indianapolis, either. He said one day it would be a fine town, maybe even as important as Cincinnati. It was the state capital. Already it had a few factories, and mills for paper, flour, and wool. There were churches, a variety of shops, and a post office.

"It will grow fast, just like you boys," he told his sons. "Mark my words! Mark my words!" Until early this year, Father had been a state senator. He was proud of the city and state.

El's boots made a satisfying rasping sound as he scuffed them along the wooden walk in front of Caleb Simon's cooper shop. Through the doorway he could see a pile of barrel hoops stacked inside, next to the finished barrels the cooper had made.

El decided to go home by way of the Circle, which marked the center of town. He stopped to look at the large house that sat in the middle of a scraggly lawn ringed by Circle Street. Though the house was built to be the governor's mansion, the governor—Noah Noble—chose to live in his own house on a farm east of town.

Three blocks east of the Circle, on Ohio Street, was El's home. Here, away from busy Washington Street, the houses were spaced far apart. Neat-looking picket fences marked most of the property lines.

He went through the gate of the whitewashed picket fence in front of his house. In the dull light of the late afternoon, the red frame house was a welcoming sight. He followed the dirt path around to the rear, past the kitchen, a small frame building nestled close to the house. Beyond was Mother's garden and a large woodlot that belonged to Father.

El quickly scraped the mud off his shoes before stepping onto the back porch. As he moved, pain stabbed through the joints of his swollen fingers, and his nose ached again.

El could hear his two-year-old brother, Stoughton, calling Mother in the sitting room. Maria, his baby sister, was probably napping. His two other younger brothers were not here. Mother had not been feeling well, so seven-year-old Calvin was staying with Mother's brother, Uncle James Hill, and his wife, Aunt Maria. Five-year-old Miles was up in Noblesville with the Fletchers' good friend Mr. Mallory. Miles went to school in Mr. Mallory's home.

As El opened the sitting-room door, he heard Mother.

"Stoughton," she scolded, "stay back from the fireplace. I've told you before to mind the sparks." Mother had little patience with those who, told once, forgot the second time.

"Mother," El called loudly as he hurried into the room.

"Elijah!" Mother said sharply. She squared her shoulders and looked down at him with an unsmiling face. Slowly she folded her hands in front of her long black skirt. Her tight-fitting bodice with its high collar made her seem even taller and thinner than she was.

"Mind your manners," she continued. "It's rude to rush into a room that

way. And it's very unlike you to be rude, Elijah. Now, what have you been up to? Just look at your nose!"

El hung his head. "It happened at school today." The anger he had felt came flooding back. He showed her his swollen hand.

"We will put this to rights," she said firmly. "Then you can tell me what happened."

She took El into the large bedroom where she and Father slept, next to the dining room. Maria was asleep in her cradle close by the bed. Mother poured water from a pitcher into the small washbowl that sat on top of the chest of drawers. Quickly but carefully, she cleaned El's cuts and bruises.

While she worked the words came from El in a rush. "I was copying my spelling words into my copybook. Then I dropped ink on the page. I blotted it as best I could with my pen rag. But the blot was still there, big and dark. I licked it to make it go away, but that just made it worse."

His cheeks smarted as he remembered how Cooley had laughed at him. He was tempted to tell Mother, but decided not to. He wasn't a tattler.

"Schoolmaster Gregg came along and saw the blot in my copybook," El went on. "He cracked my nose with the ferule when he hit at my hand. It—it just sort of got in the way. But it wasn't right for him to give me such a hard punishment!" El complained angrily. "My marks are almost as high as Cooley's, and he's the best in the school."

Mother shook her head in disapproval when El mentioned the ferule. "Your father is out of town on business. As soon as he returns tomorrow, I will talk with him about this schoolmaster."

El's voice trembled as he fought back tears. "Mother, I don't want to go to school anymore. I'll just read a lot and teach myself." He loved to read, though Cooley teased him and called him a bookworm.

Mother put her hand underneath his chin and looked directly into his eyes. "Elijah, you know how important your father and I think a good education is. It will take educated men to build our new town and state. And, Elijah, without schooling you may not have the kind of life you want."

"I don't care!" El cried.

Mother looked at El out of the corner of her eye. After a few minutes of thought she said, "Very well. Starting tomorrow you may work for me."

Though Mother had a hired girl to help her, El knew that Mother always had much to do. She had soap, candles, and butter to make. She spun, sewed, cooked, and washed. She looked after the hog killing. And she saw to it that all the meat was salted and hung up and smoked in its proper time. In the spring she made maple sugar and syrup.

There was plenty Mother could have him do, besides his daily chores. He guessed that tomorrow he would find out what she had in mind.

TWO
Wood Chips

Early the next morning, Mother put El to work picking up the wood chips from trees that had been felled and chopped into logs. The chips would smolder nicely when burned in the smokehouse, where she cured hams for the family's meals.

After breakfast he pulled on his wool coat and hat. He took a wooden pail that sat near the back door and went out to the woodlot beyond the small garden.

Across the street were several frame houses and an abandoned log cabin. Father said it wouldn't be long before frame and brick would take the place of the town's log buildings. Some of the churches and a few other buildings were made of brick. And William Conner had already built a large brick house on his large farm near Noblesville.

The air felt cold and damp on El's cheeks, and overhead low, gray clouds crept from east to west. In the woodlot he found wood chips scattered every-

where. He had not noticed before how many wood chips were left over when you made a neat stack of logs.

The scent of damp, fallen leaves mixed with the heavy smell of woodsmoke. El thought the air outside smelled ever so much better than Mr. Gregg's stuffy schoolroom. Quickly he began to scoop up the chips.

As he worked, El thought of Cooley, bent over his copybook at school. He imagined the singsong drone of scholars reciting their lessons. But here in the woodlot he heard only the rattle of wagon wheels bumping over the muddy ruts of the nearby street, the muffled sounds of horses' hooves, and the shouted greetings from passersby on Ohio Street.

How much better it was to be free! El thought. His nose and hand felt much better today. Eagerly he scooped up more chips and dumped them into the pail.

He worked steadily, carrying pail after pail of chips to a pile near the smoke-house. At first the hours went quickly. But by noon his arms ached and the pail seemed heavier with each trip. The damp cold seeped through his trousers and coat, and he was chilled.

When dinnertime came at noon the warmth of the house felt good. After dinner he slipped a favorite book into his coat pocket. It was one of a famous series of books for young people by Peter Parley, *The Tales of Peter Parley About America.* Maybe he could read just a page or two later on, when he needed to rest his arms.

By midafternoon his trips to the chip pile took longer and longer. Finally he sat down behind the barn, out of sight of the house, and opened his book.

As he read, his eyelids gradually got heavier and heavier. Before he knew it, the book fell from his hands and he dozed off.

When he opened his eyes, he saw a pair of feet standing in front of him. Blinking the sleep from his eyes, he looked up. Mother was staring down at him.

"Elijah, if a boy agrees to do a day's labor he must work till suppertime, not read."

"Yes, Mother." El jumped to his feet and jammed the book into his coat pocket.

"I will not tolerate laziness," she added with a shake of her head.

Though Mother did not look strong, she could work from dawn to dusk without complaint, El knew. And she expected everyone else to do the same.

He reached down for the empty pail. His muscles were stiff, and he had never felt so tired.

The next morning El was slower than Cooley getting out of bed. Outside it was not yet light, and the wood floor of their room felt rough and cold to his bare feet.

"Come on, lazybones!" Cooley called. "Father will be halfway through devotions before you get your chores done." He banged down the stairs and out the back door.

El knew he would catch it if he was late for the Bible reading and prayers before breakfast. But first the horses must be fed and brushed, the stable cleaned, and the wood brought into the house and neatly stacked by the fireplaces and stove.

He pulled on his clothes and ran down the narrow stairs. He glanced through the open doorway of his parents' room as he headed toward the back door. Father was still at his desk. Almost every morning he wrote in his diary. He wrote about his business and his family and the weather. After he finished writing, he inspected the barn and the smokehouse before breakfast.

El hurried through his chores and arrived back in the house, out of breath, just in time for devotions. After breakfast, he watched Cooley run off to school and thought of his own long, boring day ahead. Maybe Mother was right after all, he thought. Though he hated Schoolmaster Gregg, he had never found school boring.

At last he decided to talk to his parents. He found them in the sitting room, planning the day's work.

"Mother, Father, could I please speak with you?"

"Yes," Mother answered. "But be quick about it. Your father must soon be off to his law office, and I have a basket of food to take over to Widow Wilkins. She's taken poorly again, pour soul, and is very sick."

Father rose and turned toward El, his hands clasped behind his back. His thick dark hair framed a square, strong-looking face. The pleats in his spotless white shirt were perfectly pressed, and his black coat and trousers had been freshly brushed clean by Mother.

"What is the order of the day, young man?" Father's voice was deep and his speech was quick. "There's a long day's work to be done, and no reading or sleeping along the way."

El hung his head. "Yes, Father. Mother, Father," he began, hesitating. "I've decided I would like to go back to school."

Father raised his eyebrows.

"You have changed your mind, Elijah?" Mother asked, a thoughtful tone to her voice.

"Yes." El looked first at Father, then at Mother.

Father nodded his head. "So you have decided that you want to be a scholar again? Very sensible." He looked at Mother. "But under the right schoolmaster, eh?"

Mother nodded her head, to El's surprise. There was the hint of a smile on her face as she looked at him.

"Boys need a touch of the ferule now and then, Elijah," Father went on. "But you have the makings of a good scholar and would do better under the right teacher, we believe. I have someone in mind, a Mrs. Kent, who runs an academy in Greenwood. We will talk this over tonight. The end of the term is not far away, and the change could be made then."

El had never heard of Mrs. Kent's Academy. But if he was allowed to change schools, he planned to show Mother and Father just how good a scholar he could be—maybe even better than Cooley! This was the sort of hard work he didn't mind.

THREE

A Farewell

Early in March of 1834, El and his mother set out for Mrs. Kent's Academy in Greenwood, a small village about ten miles south of town. Father could not go with them. Instead he sent his brother, El's Uncle Stoughton, along.

El, dressed in his best clothes and with a new broad-brimmed hat on, clung tightly to Mother's waist as he rode behind her. Her cream-colored horse, Pomp, trotted along at a smart pace in the crisp, springlike air. Tall, budding trees pressed close to the edge of the narrow road that led southward from Indianapolis. Only a few scattered farms lay along its path. Much of the way was through dense forest.

El saw moving shadows on the forest floor as the sparkling sunlight filtered down through the trees' high branches. Little flecks of white trillium and patches of purple violets poked through last fall's blanket of fallen leaves. These wildflowers were scattered throughout the forest as far as El could see. It all smelled wonderfully fresh to El.

Every now and then, over the steady, soft drumming of the horses' hooves on the packed clay of the road, El could hear rustlings in the forest. He imagined wild animals hiding in the moving shadows, waiting, ready to pounce. A bear, or maybe a panther? he wondered. He was glad to have hold of Mother and to know Uncle Stoughton was following close behind.

The damp, rich smell of the forest reminded El of the day he and Mother had ridden together down another road until they came to a stand of beautiful oaks. Surrounding the oaks was open, gently rolling land where people from a church

in Indianapolis were holding a camp meeting. Folks came from miles around to attend, even if they were not members of this church.

They listened to sermons and prayed and sang all day long. El remembered how good the singing made him feel. The sweet melodies of the hymns were pleasant to his ears, and the words of the preachers were powerful and moving. El thought maybe he would like to be a preacher someday.

A sudden shout from Uncle Stoughton interrupted El's daydream.

"Look here, Elijah! Wild turkey tracks, right alongside the road."

El nodded excitedly and slid sideways on Pomp to see the turkey tracks. Not far back they had seen hoofprints of deer.

He loosened his hold on Mother so he could lean out farther. But Pomp's shiny coat was slick, and El lost his balance. He slid off Pomp's back and landed with a thud on the dusty road. His new hat landed on a bush.

Pomp's rear hoof narrowly missed stepping on him. Only Mother's quick action and firm hands on the reins kept the mare from bolting.

El bounced to his feet, but he could see by the look on Mother's face that she was not pleased. He hurried to fetch his hat.

"Elijah," she scolded, "what am I going to do with you? You must learn to think before you act."

Uncle Stoughton threw his head back and laughed.

Mother looked disapprovingly in Uncle Stoughton's direction. He quickly dismounted and helped El climb up behind Mother again.

It was a short time later, close to noon, when they reached Greenwood. All the small village's cluster of buildings were made of logs. But on the outskirts was a white frame house with a neat, white picket fence around it. Not far away, surrounded by a small, open field, was another white frame building. This, Mother pointed out, was Mrs. Kent's Academy.

The house, El discovered, was where he would board, or live, while going to school at the academy. An older couple came out to meet them.

Mother had explained to El that they were friends of Mrs. Kent and known to Father. They came from Vermont, as did Mrs. Kent. El was to call them Aunt Patsy and Uncle Henry, though they were not really relatives.

"Dinner will be ready soon," Aunt Patsy said, after greeting them with a big smile. She was short and fat, and her voice was loud and jolly-sounding. "Just come in and set a spell," she called over her shoulder as she bustled out toward the kitchen.

El, who suddenly felt very hungry, dropped his hat on the chair behind him and started to follow Aunt Patsy to the kitchen.

"Elijah," Mother said quickly. "Mind your manners. Sit down and wait until you're called to the table."

Without thinking, El promptly sat down. Too late, he felt his hat crumple beneath him. Hurriedly he jumped up and turned to rescue it. But its well-rounded crown was as flat as the chair seat, and it looked like a big black pancake.

"Now, that's a sorry sight!" Mother folded her hands in her lap and looked sternly at El.

Uncle Stoughton put his hand over his mouth. El could see that he was trying not to laugh.

"Straighten it out as best you can, Elijah," Mother went on. "Crushed though it is, you'll just have to wear it. Waste not, want not," she added firmly.

"Yes, Mother." El felt his cheeks grow hot with embarrassment.

El forgot all about his hat after Aunt Patsy called them to the table. Warm, sweet-smelling corn bread was followed by a platter heaped with steaming fried chicken and a big bowl of potatoes. El had a large helping of potatoes, two large chunks of corn bread spread thickly with honey, and four chicken legs. He picked the bones so clean that Mother again had to remind him of his manners.

After dinner El and Mother walked over to the academy, while Uncle Stoughton visited with Aunt Patsy and Uncle Henry. As they walked along, El wondered about Mrs. Kent's school. Would it be as big as Schoolmaster Gregg's? What would Mrs. Kent look like? Was she old or young?

El could hear the jumbled sounds of the scholars reciting their lessons as he and Mother reached the building. Mother knocked at the door. Suddenly the droning voices stopped. The door swung open, and there stood a short, stocky woman about Mother's age. Her black hair was drawn back from her face and rolled into a neat bun at the back of her head.

Her dark, smiling eyes and round cheeks gave her a friendly look. Quickly, she invited Mother and El inside.

"Good afternoon. You must be Mrs. Fletcher. I'm Mrs. Frances Kent. And this must be Elijah! Welcome to our school."

Her voice sounded warm and friendly. El breathed a sigh of relief.

"Girls, boys," Mrs. Kent announced. "This is your new schoolmate, Elijah Fletcher. He has come to us all the way from Indianapolis."

A few of the children wriggled in their seats, a few smiled at him, and several waved to catch his attention. El felt too shy to move, yet soon he found himself seated by another boy his age.

After talking briefly with Mrs. Kent, Mother gave El a quick good-bye and left.

This gave El an awful empty feeling in his stomach, a feeling that he had never had before. For the first time in his life, he realized, he was alone among strangers. There wasn't a single person from his family nearby—not for miles around.

FOUR

Homesick

"Get it, El!" Newton shouted.

"Yeah, get it if you can, city boy!" Jason teased.

The wooden ball came hurling bumpily over the field. El raised his long, flattened stick and swung as hard as he could. There was a loud *smack* as the stick connected solidly with the ball. El's shot sped along the ground toward the goal at the end of the field. He ran as fast as he could, following it. Out of the corner of his eye he saw Jason and his teammates run to block him.

In a final burst of speed, he reached the ball. Guiding it with his stick, he ran toward the two stones that marked the goal. With Jason close on his heels, he gave the ball a final push. It went neatly between the goal stones, scoring a point for his side.

"Yahoo!" shouted Newton. "You're doing great, El!"

El grinned. There was no doubt about it. During the past weeks in Green-

wood, he had become a good shinny player. And he had made friends with
Newton and several other boys his age.

He was doing well at his studies, too. Yet he still felt homesick sometimes,
especially on weekends.

Father wrote that Uncle Stoughton would fetch him home from Greenwood
for a visit in a few weeks. But El was impatient. A few weeks seemed a long way
off. He didn't see why he couldn't make the journey by himself. That would
give Jason something to think about!

After the game, as he walked home to Aunt Patsy's, he thought of a plan.
Tomorrow was Friday. He would act on his plan this weekend.

The next day, the April weather was warm and springlike. The sky was clear
and sunny. But the dark of night would come shortly after suppertime. After
school was out for the day, El knew he must hurry. There would be only a few
hours of daylight left.

26

He wrote a note to Aunt Patsy on his school slate, saying he was going home for the weekend. Then he propped the slate on the rocking chair in the kitchen. He wanted to be well on his way before she or Uncle Henry got home.

"She'll be sure to see it here when she comes in," El said to himself.

Water stood in the ruts and low spots in the road from yesterday's rain. So El carried his shoes and socks for safekeeping. Soon he was out of sight of the village. He passed by a few open fields and several log cabins. He could hear the cooing pigeons and the evensongs of other birds as he neared the forest.

It seemed much darker than he remembered it. Overhead the young, pale green leaves let only fragments of the fading sunlight peek through. His bare feet scarcely made a noise on the mud-caked road. He could hear the faint sounds of unknown creatures stirring here and there among the trees.

There was a rustling in a bush. Then without warning there came a terrifying screech from off to his left, not far into the woods. The screech turned into a series of yowls and cries.

Clutching his shoes to his chest, El ran as fast as he could. It was a long way to the next clearing, he remembered. But then he fought back the feeling of fear. Surely a bear or a panther wouldn't make such sounds, especially before it attacked? He made himself slow down to a walk and continue on as before. At last he reached the clearing. Luck was with him! Ahead he saw the tail end of a farm wagon disappearing down the road.

He ran after it. When he got close enough, he called out. "Halloo, halloo!" Hanging tightly onto his shoes with one hand, he waved wildly with the other.

The driver turned and looked over his shoulder. "Whoa!" he called to his team of horses. The wagon stopped, and the driver motioned to El. "Come on, young 'un. I ain't got all day."

Breathless, El climbed up onto the wagon seat beside the farmer.

"You look like you bit into a green persimmon," the driver remarked, giving El a sidewise glance. El explained about the cry in the forest.

The farmer slapped his knee, laughing. "Why, that was just a little old owl! Makes a powerful lot of noise. Don't usually hear them this time of day."

El felt a little foolish. At least he had stopped running, he told himself.

It was well past candle-lighting time before El reached home. The golden glow of light through the windows was the most welcoming sight he had ever seen.

With a shouted "I'm home!" El banged open the back door. He could see Mother and Father in the sitting room. He guessed that his brothers were upstairs in bed. Baby Maria would be asleep in Mother and Father's room.

Surprised, Father looked up from his newspaper, and Mother dropped her book into her lap.

"Well, young man," Father said, frowning. "What's the meaning of this? You haven't run away from school, have you?"

"No, Father," El hurried to answer. "It's just that I . . . Well, sir, the truth is I got homesick. And I wanted to show Jason at school that I wasn't a city boy afraid of the woods."

"Elijah, it was foolish of you to travel alone," Mother scolded. "Something dreadful might have happened to you."

"You must not travel alone through the forest at night," Father agreed. "But you *are* growing up, Elijah. It is time you did more things on your own."

Encouraged, El explained that a farmer had given him a ride all the way to Indianapolis. "But I lost one of my socks when I ran to catch my ride with him," El confessed.

"I wouldn't expect that of a boy who receives such good reports from Mrs. Kent," Father said.

"I like having Mrs. Kent as a teacher," El said enthusiastically. "But sometimes I miss home—especially now that we have Maria."

Mother's face softened as she looked at El. "You boys do seem to enjoy having a sister. I must be careful that you don't spoil Maria."

El was surprised to see one of Father's rare smiles at the mention of Maria. But he was even more surprised when Mother gave him a good-night hug. It gave him a nice warm feeling inside to be home again.

FIVE

Cooley's Bump

Blue-white lightning filled the room with a blinding flash and made the sleeping faces of Cooley, Miles, Stoughton, and Calvin appear ghostly and unreal. Abruptly there was a boom of thunder. Then there was another flash of lightning, followed by a deep-throated growl of thunder rolling off into the distance.

El sat up straight on the featherbed that he shared with Cooley. His body was rigid and his eyes were wide with fear.

"I'm dead—I'm dead!" he screamed.

Cooley propped himself up on one elbow. "El, what's all the ruckus about?" he grumbled sleepily.

Stoughton and Calvin didn't stir, but Miles woke and began to whimper.

"Now look what you've done," Cooley went on. "Just wait until I tell Mother what a 'fraidy cat you are."

"Don't you dare, Cooley." El was wide awake now. He realized he had been dreaming. The thunder and lightning of the July storm had become part of his dream.

Outside their second-floor bedroom window, El could see the trees swaying in the wind. They made strange shadow shapes on the walls when the lightning flashed.

El got up and groped his way over to where Miles lay. "It's all right, Miles. I was just having a bad dream. Go back to sleep."

"I want Mother," Miles protested. But El persuaded him to close his eyes, and soon he drifted off to sleep again.

El remembered how he had felt about storms when he was very young. He had been terrified of them, though Cooley never was. Once when he was three years old there was a terrible storm, and Mother came and sang to him. It had made his fright go away.

"You won't tell on me, will you, Cooley?" El whispered, as he crawled back in bed again.

Cooley thought for a minute. "Not if you promise to play soldiers with me tomorrow and do exactly as I say."

"All right," El agreed, hoping Cooley would forget about the promise. He'd been glad when spring term ended and he could come home for the summer. But he found his brother hadn't changed his bossy ways.

By morning the rain had stopped. But the sky was a dull gray, like Mother's pewter plates. The air was hot and heavy. It was a good day to find a cool spot and read, El thought.

After chores were done and breakfast was over, Calvin, Stoughton, and Miles headed toward the barn to play. But Cooley shouted to El, "I'm the captain! Follow me, soldier." He put on a paper hat he had made and shouldered a long stick that was his rifle.

The wind picked up and the sky darkened. Cooley had to hold the hat on with one hand as he led the way across the street.

"Where are we going, Cooley?" El wanted to know.

"Just you wait and see," Cooley answered, still playacting. He led El toward the abandoned log cabin. Behind it was a small barn, and scattered in the barnyard were a few broken wheels and an old wagon bed.

The neighbor's old hound dog, Trapper, greeted them with wagging tail. Uninvited, Trapper tagged along after El.

"Here." Cooley stopped. "I'll stand guard at the cabin. It can be our fort. You go over to the barn and scout around for unfriendly Indians."

A strong gust of wind picked up the loose wooden roof shingles on the cabin. Some of them went sailing off down the street. Suddenly the sky grew much darker.

"Cooley, I think it's going to storm again. We'd better get back home."

" 'Fraidy cat!" Cooley teased. "It'll blow over. Do as I say, El. You promised." Cooley took up his post by the door of the log cabin.

By now the wind was blowing steady and hard. The sky took on a strange, muddy yellow color, and Trapper ran toward the barn for shelter. With a glance at the sky, El ran after the dog.

Suddenly the air became very quiet. Trapper began to whimper and whine. El bent down and patted him on the head. "What's the matter, old boy?" he asked. "I've heard tell you can sense danger when humans can't." He watched Cooley, who was marching back and forth close to the cabin.

"Cooley, you'd better get over here," El shouted from the barn. "This weather's weird!" He had scarcely got the words out when there was a great rush of wind.

From the shelter of the barn, he could see the look of surprise on Cooley's face. Then the wind snapped an empty window frame from the cabin. It flew out and struck Cooley on the back of the head. Without a sound he crumpled to the ground.

El's stomach knotted with fear. What if Cooley was hurt really bad? For the first time in his life he prayed for his brother. The preacher at chapel said prayer helped.

Then he leaned into the wind and started toward the cabin. He got no farther than two steps when he was thrown back against the barn. He dropped to his knees and began to crawl, closing his eyes against the stinging wind. Blindly he crawled in the direction of the cabin.

At last he reached Cooley. His brother's eyes were shut and his paper hat lay crushed and bloody beneath his cheek.

El knew that Cooley needed help in a hurry. But in this wind, how was he going to get Mother? Despite his prayer, he still felt afraid. Then the wind stopped as suddenly as it had begun. He didn't waste any time, but raced for home as fast as he could go.

"Cooley's hurt! Cooley's hurt!" he screamed as he ran into the sitting room. Without stopping to ask questions, Mother followed El to where Cooley lay.

The hair on the back of Cooley's head was matted with blood. But he was awake, moaning in pain.

"Will Cooley be all right, Mother?" El asked, frightened.

"We'll see," Mother answered. Her tone was steady, but she had a worried look on her face. Between them they carried Cooley home.

Mother put cooling compresses on his head and cleaned the wound. Then she sat by his bedside while he rested.

Later that day, Mother told El that Cooley would be all right.

When Father came home, he said that the storm had been a tornado. A few streets away, it had blown a tree down and lifted the roof off a small house. El thought Cooley had been pretty lucky. He guessed his prayers had been answered.

SIX

Watermelons

The next day El hurried toward the other side of town with two loaves of freshly baked bread tucked under one arm. Mother had asked him to deliver them to Widow Wilkins. The widow was feeling poorly again, with the chills and fever of the ague, and Mother wanted to make sure she was all right after yesterday's tornado.

El wanted to see what damage the storm had done, so he decided to go west on Washington Street. Cooley had wanted to come, too. But Mother said he had to stay in bed for the day, though the bump on his head looked smaller.

Soon El reached the wide open space where the new State House was being built. It seemed to El the builders were taking forever to put it up. It was going to be two stories high, with tall white columns all along its front and a dome on its top. This would be the grandest building in Indiana when it was finished. Inside there would even be room for a state library.

As El neared White River the street became clogged with wagons, coaches,

and ox carts. In the summer there always was a lot of traffic on the National Road. At the new covered bridge, the slow-moving vehicles stopped. They had to pay a toll before rumbling their way across its wooden deck. To El the bridge looked like a giant barn that had been stretched to about four times its usual length. It had plank sides and a wooden roof, and rested on huge stone pillars. Father said it was one of the wonders of the state.

After taking a close look at the bridge, El hurried on to Widow Wilkins's. He was surprised to see that this part of town hadn't been touched by the tornado.

He hoped he would not have to stay and visit at the Widow's. She liked to talk a lot.

Despite her ague, she made El come in. "This July heat's enough to get a body down," she complained. "So you just come in and set a spell before you go back."

"But, Widow Wilkins . . ." El began.

Widow Wilkins paid no attention to El's words. "You know, I've been living right here for almost fourteen years—since the very beginning of this town—and I've never seen such miserable hot times."

"I know, Widow Wilkins. . . ."

Again Widow Wilkins went right on talking. "There were about fifteen families that really got the settlement going. Things were a mite different than they are now." A faraway look came to her eyes.

El remembered Mother's stories about early times in Indianapolis. Mother and Father, their hired Conestoga wagon piled high with furniture and belongings, had come to Indianapolis from Ohio. They arrived a few years before Cooley was born in April 1823. At first they lived in a log cabin on the west side of town. Then they moved to a small frame house on Washington Street, where El was born in 1824. The Fletchers had not moved to their present home on Ohio Street until 1831.

At last El was able to get away from Widow Wilkins. But he had to agree with her about the weather. The hazy July sun had never felt so hot, and the heavy traffic on Washington Street just made it worse. He decided to go home by a less-traveled way, through a large, partly wooded section north of Washington Street.

As El walked north and east, the coolness of the trees gave way to Ohio Street. Here there were only a few buildings, and the houses were spaced well apart.

One of them was an old, deserted-looking log cabin with its door sagging open. Next to the cabin was a patch of watermelons with row after row of melons peeking through the vines. El could almost taste the sweet, juicy pulp.

He ran over to the patch, stooped down, and gave one of the watermelons a thump with his knuckles. There was a nice hollow sound.

"It looks like no one lives here anymore," El said to himself. "And these melons must be just about ripe enough to eat."

Without thinking any more about it, he took the pocket knife Father had given him for Christmas and cut a plug in one. Disappointed, he saw that it was not yet ripe. Thirstier than ever, he hurried to the next melon and cut a plug in it.

Suddenly a man's deep voice shouted, "Stop! Young 'un, you got no business in my melon patch."

El turned, his eyes wide with surprise. Standing in the cabin's doorway was a tall black man. His white shaggy eyebrows were pulled down in a frown, and his bushy white hair framed the strong features of his face. El recognized him: Harry Wright, a freed slave from Tennessee, known to Father.

"El Fletcher, we're going to see your father right now."

Suddenly El realized the mistake he had made. Someone did live in the cabin—Harry! He tried to explain to Harry, but the words just wouldn't come. He could see Harry was in no notion of listening, either. Father would likely give El a good switching for spoiling Harry's melons.

When he and Harry reached the Fletchers', Father has just arrived home from his office. Angrily Harry told Father about El's mischief. Father listened carefully.

"I'll take care of this, Harry," Father said. "You did the right thing by coming directly to me."

"All right, Mr. Fletcher," Harry answered with a nod. "I'll be on my way then."

At last El was able to speak. "But, Father, I didn't know anyone lived in that cabin. Besides, it was just old Harry. . . ."

"Elijah! You should be ashamed of yourself. A big boy of nearly ten!" Father's voice was filled with anger and his fists were clenched behind his back. He studied El for a long moment.

El could almost feel the sting of the switch on the seat of his pants. At last Father spoke.

"Before I decide what your punishment should be, I'm going to tell you a story. It's a case—a legal argument—about slavery. It took place right here in Indianapolis. You must decide which side you would defend."

"You mean if I was a lawyer like you?"

"Yes, Elijah."

"But slavery is against the law in Indiana. So how could there be a case about slavery in Indianapolis?"

Father looked pleased at El's remark. "You have a quick mind, Elijah, but listen to my story. Now, what happened was this. A slaveowner came to Indianapolis from Virginia. He brought with him four slaves—a black woman and her three young children. The man was traveling westward, beyond the state of Indiana. But because of bad weather, he had to spend several days here in town.

"While here, the slave woman learned that Indiana was a free state. She believed she was now free, so she took her three children and left the slave-owner. He claimed they still belonged to him, though they were passing through a free state. The woman refused to return to him. So an Indiana judge was asked to hear the case."

"When did this happen, Father?" El wanted to know.

"Five years ago—in eighteen twenty-nine. It was the first time Indiana, as a free state, was asked to legally protect the rights of blacks in its courts. Which side would you choose, Elijah?"

El thought for a minute. "I don't think slavery is right. And I'm sorry for what I did. I would want to speak for the slaves."

"Well chosen, Elijah," said Father, with an approving nod. "That's what I did, though some folks didn't thank me for it. And I won the case. The slaves went free under Indiana law."

"Now I understand why you were angry, Father," El said. "I never stopped to think."

"I can see you've learned a valuable lesson, Elijah," Father said thoughtfully.

40

"I've decided to take that knife away from you, until you learn to use it properly. Instead of a switching, you can repay Harry. You can help harvest his melons, then help him sell them on the market."

"Yes, Father," El quickly agreed.

"You have a good head on your shoulders, Elijah. But like that knife, you must learn to use it to good purpose."

El thought that working for Harry was much better than getting a switching. But it hurt to lose his knife.

SEVEN

Cincinnati

The driver gave his whip a sharp snap. With a lurch the stagecoach started its journey.

El had just turned eleven, and he was the envy of his friends. Travel by stage was not to be taken lightly. It was expensive and sometimes dangerous, especially on the fast mail-coaches. He felt puffed up about going by stage to Cincinnati, even though this coach was not one of the mail-coaches.

This was a trip that Father had promised him and Cooley and Calvin. But shortly before El's birthday this August, Calvin had come down with a fever and the shakes—the ague, Mother said—and had to stay home.

El leaned out the window to watch the horses as they strained against the weight of the coach. Their harnesses were studded with highly polished brass bells. They jingled gaily as the horses trotted along.

Whenever the coach approached a town, the driver would raise his horn and

blow it as loudly as he could. This let people know the stage was coming. The tired horses would perk up and bring the stage rolling smartly up to the tavern.

People regarded the driver as a man of importance. Some thought he was more worth listening to than the schoolmaster. He carried gossip and news from town to town a lot faster than the newspapers, which were the only other way word got around.

Cooley said he would like to be a mail-coach driver so he could race on the National Road. The drivers tried to outdo one another in speeding the mail across the countryside. Relay stations supplied fresh horses, and at times the rivalry caused tempers to flare.

The coach lines that carried only passengers tried to better one another in looks. Some had elegant crimson red upholstery, with brightly painted trim on the outside of the coach. Some could carry as many as nine passengers and were pulled by six-horse teams.

But no matter how fancy they looked, coaches were a rough and uncomfortable way to travel, most people thought. Uncle Stoughton joked about this, saying he once was on a coach that got mired down in the mud. " 'All first-class passengers, get out and walk,' ordered the driver," Uncle Stoughton said. " 'All second-class passengers, get out and push.' "

By the end of the first day's travel, El had to agree that it was a pretty bumpy ride. At least he didn't have to get out and push.

It was almost suppertime on the second day of their journey when the coach reached Cincinnati.

El had never seen such sights. The city, on the banks of the mighty Ohio River, rose up from the waterfront on a terraced hillside. The terraces looked like giant steps. At the bottom of the hill was the bustling, crowded waterfront with docks and a boatyard.

One step up from the waterfront was the heart of the city. There were office buildings, hotels, banks, churches, and a bazaar. The city also had a hospital, theaters, a museum, and a college. Two- and three-story brick homes lined the streets above the busiest part of the city.

Traffic on the lower part of the hill was always busy. There were fancy-looking carriages and fashionably dressed ladies, clumsy-looking freight wagons and travel-worn stagecoaches.

El stood and stared, wide-eyed.

"El, you look like someone fresh from the backwoods, gawking away," Cooley teased.

"Well, at least I don't put on airs like you do!" El said hotly. It stung to be called a backwoodsman. He was proud of how well he did at school and of his family's place in town. Both Mother and Father were thought of highly.

"Boys!" Father said sternly. "Take your carpetbags in hand and follow me now."

He led the way to their lodgings at the Pearl Street House. It was just a short way from where the stage made its stop. This is where he stayed when he came to Cincinnati. This time he was here on bank business, for not long ago he had been made one of the bank's directors.

Father did a lot of traveling. In July he had journeyed to Fort Wayne, Indiana, for a celebration, the opening of the Wabash and Erie Canal between Fort Wayne and Huntington. Sometimes El and Cooley took turns pretending they were Father—traveling around as a lawyer to the courts in Indiana, or going beyond the boundaries of the state on important business. But this was no imagined journey. They really *had* traveled beyond the boundaries of the state.

The next morning, Sunday, Father woke the boys at six-thirty. "The first order of the day, boys," he said in a firm tone, "is early church. Then breakfast. Then midday church service."

"What about seeing the waterfront?" Cooley wanted to know.

El was anxious to see the waterfront, too. But more than anything he wanted to visit the large bookstore Father had told them about. It would be open tomorrow.

"We'll get to everything, all in good time," said Father. "I want you to see and learn as much as you can this week. Travel is bound to broaden your young minds," he added with a nod.

El sighed. Sometimes Father expected so much!

After they put on their best clothes, Father took them to a nearby church. He said it was one of the finest new buildings in the city. Then he took them to the Cincinnati Hotel for breakfast. He met some businessmen he knew and spent a long time talking with them. El tried to keep from fidgeting.

At last Father said good-bye to his friends, and he and the boys started down the hill. Eagerly they ran ahead of him as they neared the waterfront.

The first vessel they saw was a steamboat tied up at one of the docks. It was powered by a large paddle wheel, much taller than Father, that was mounted on the far side of the boat. Flat-bottomed, it looked as if it was sitting on top of the water.

As they drew close to the steamboat, El recognized the name painted on its bow—*Ellen Douglas*. He had read about it in the newspaper. It was one of the sixty-two new steamboats put on the river last year, according to the newspaper.

"May we come down and watch the boat leave tomorrow, Father?" Cooley asked eagerly, after he read the schedule posted near the gangplank.

"Yes, Father, could we?" El put in.

Father looked thoughtful. "I must take care of business in the morning. But you could learn something about the city on your own. The docks are a very busy place, though. You must stay clear of the traffic."

"We'll stay out of the way, Father," El promised.

At last Father agreed to let the boys come down to the docks in the morning. The *Ellen Douglas* was due to leave for Louisville fairly early. Perhaps the traffic wouldn't be much heavier than it was now, he said.

Traffic on the river was light because it was Sunday, but there were other boats. They saw a keelboat with a sail and several flatboats floating downriver. There was a rowboat pulled up on shore near the main dock. A boatman leaned, resting, on a post nearby. Father explained the man's boat was a ferryboat. People could pay to ride to the other side of the river.

That night before the boys went to bed, Father gave each of them two gold coins. "You are free to spend them as you wish," he said.

"Thank you, Father!" they chorused.

To El, tomorrow seemed like a very promising day.

EIGHT

The Steamboat

Early the next morning, El and Cooley hurried along the busy streets, down the hill to the waterfront. First they would watch the *Ellen Douglas* depart. Then Father said they could visit the shops. El wanted to buy the latest Peter Parley book. Cooley wasn't sure how he wanted to spend his money. He thought he might buy new watercolor paints, or maybe he would buy a travel book.

At the dock where the steamboat was tied up, passengers were arriving on foot and in buggies. Leather trunks, hatboxes, and odd-shaped carpetbags were being carried aboard.

El shrank out of the way to avoid being bumped or shouted at.

"Come on, El," Cooley urged, his eyes shining with excitement. "Let's go on board and take a quick look."

El was tempted, but he shook his head. "You know Father said only passengers were allowed on board."

"Aw, nobody's going to care as long as we get off before it leaves," Cooley argued. "Don't be a stick-in-the-mud, El."

"I'm not coming," El said stubbornly. Sometimes doing the right thing was hard, especially around Cooley.

"You'll just have to wait here, then, until I get back." With that, Cooley dashed on ahead.

El watched as his brother weaved in and out among the passengers and crewmen on the dock. He worked his way toward the gangplank, where one of the crew was collecting money for tickets. Quickly Cooley slipped behind the crewman's back, up the short gangplank, and onto the deck. Then El lost sight of him.

Soon El could hear the rhythmic chugging of the engine. The crowd around the gangplank thinned, then disappeared. It looked as if the boat was getting ready to leave. El began to wonder where Cooley was. Then there was a sudden blast on the boat's whistle.

El watched in alarm as the crew pulled the gangplank on board. Ropes holding the boat to the dock were loosened and coiled onto the deck. The great paddle wheel began to turn. Slowly the *Ellen Douglas* pulled away from the dock and headed toward the middle of the river. Once it reached the deep channel there, it would turn downstream toward Louisville.

Suddenly Cooley appeared at the stern of the boat. He was jumping up and down, shouting and waving in El's direction.

El felt he had to do something—anything—to get Cooley off the boat. But what? Then he caught sight of the ferryman they had seen yesterday. His rowboat was small and slow-going. But it would take time for the steamboat to reach midstream, then turn downriver. If the ferryman rowed hard, he might be able to head the steamboat off before it got up to speed.

El saw it as his only chance. He ran to the boatman.

"Please," he cried, "I must catch the steamboat!" He held one of his gold coins out to the ferryman. In a rush he explained about Cooley.

The ferryman shook his head. "I doubt if we can catch her, but for gold I'd

give most anything a try." He shoved off and started pulling hard and rhyth-mically on the oars.

El anxiously watched the *Ellen Douglas* steam slowly toward midstream. Then he saw it almost come to a stop. Now he could no longer hear the throbbing of the engine.

"Well, I'll be hornswoggled!" cried the ferryman. "She's stopped. Must be her engine gave out. Happens every now and then." He bent over his oars and began rowing again, harder than ever. Gradually the gap between the rowboat and the steamboat narrowed.

Now El could see inside the steamboat's wheelhouse, which sat atop the cabins on the upper deck. There was Cooley! He seemed to be talking to the captain, who was at the wheel. Cooley pointed toward El and the rowboat. The captain reached for the whistle cord and gave it several pulls.

"He's signaling—he's signaling!" El cried.

"Well, I'll be hornswoggled!" the ferryman said again. With a few strong strokes of the oars he caught up with the steamboat and pulled alongside. The steamboat's deck was within El's reach when he stood. "Grab hold of the bottom of the railing, young 'un, so we don't drift away."

Several curious passengers watched as Cooley hurriedly climbed down from the wheelhouse and ran along the narrow deck. Just then the throb of the engine began again. With El's help, Cooley hastily climbed into the ferryboat.

Shoving an oar against the side of the steamer, the ferryman pushed clear. El heard the churning of the paddle wheel as it started to turn on the other side of the boat. Gradually the distance between the boats widened. The wake of the *Ellen Douglas* made the rowboat bob up and down. But soon it was in calmer waters and headed toward shore.

"I saw you coming, El," Cooley said excitedly. "So I ran up to the wheelhouse. I told the captain what happened—that I didn't mean to be a stowaway. He was plenty mad! Then something went wrong with the engine and he had to stop. And that's when you caught up with us!" By the time Cooley had finished his story he was out of breath.

The more El thought about the fright Cooley had given him, the angrier he got. "Cooley, you almost got into a lot of trouble, and you cost me one of the gold coins Father gave us!"

Cooley sat up as straight as he could and looked down his nose at El. "My dear brother," he said in a haughty playacting tone, "don't give it another thought. You may have all my gold," he added with a wave of his hand.

El's anger began to leave him, but he heaved a deep sigh. "Yesterday the preacher at church said we all must be our brother's keeper. But I find it's a mighty trying job with a brother like you!"

Cooley grinned and shrugged his shoulders. "I'm sorry, El."

Once safely back on shore, El took only one of Cooley's gold coins. He felt that this time maybe a little forgiveness was called for.

NINE

Buckwheat Pancakes

El and Cooley peeked through Mother's bedroom door. It was just a few days after their return from Cincinnati, and now Mother lay sick in bed. Her lips were blue. From time to time her thin body shook with chills, though the August air was still and hot.

"She looks like she's going to die," Cooley whispered in a shaky tone.

"Cooley, that's no way to talk," El said, trying to sound brave. "Lots of folks have the ague every year about this time, just like Calvin did. And he got well."

"But this is different," Cooley argued. "She was all right this morning when Father left for Noblesville. And she felt good enough to fix our supper tonight. Seems she got sick awful suddenlike."

El was more worried than he wanted to admit. He suspected Mother had not felt really well since their baby brother, Ingram, was born in June.

It was a lot of work taking care of such a big family. Luckily Ingram and

Maria were staying with Uncle Stoughton for a few days. And this morning Father had taken Calvin and Miles out to the farm Father owned to stay with Uncle James. This eased the burden on Mother.

El's thoughts were interrupted by a faint call from Mother. "Boys, come in here."

They hurried to her bedside. Stoughton was playing quietly on the floor nearby. The evening shadows made the room seem cooler than any place else in the house.

"Your father will be out of town until tomorrow evening," she began. "So you must keep an eye on Stoughton and get the meals. The supper dishes need to be washed and . . ." She seemed too tired to continue.

"Don't worry, Mother," Cooley hurried to offer.

"We'll take care of everything," El added. But he didn't feel as confident as he sounded. It had always been Mother who took care of the sick. Mother, like other frontier women, had learned to be both doctor and nurse. She cared for neighbors and friends, too, when they were ill.

"Now, see that Stoughton goes to bed right away," Mother managed to add.

"Yes, Mother," they answered.

"Come on, Stoughton," Cooley ordered.

El held out his hand for Stoughton to take. "I'll help you get washed."

"I don't want to wash," Stoughton said, a stubborn look on his face. But reluctantly he allowed El to lead him from the room. Cooley followed close behind.

A short time later, Stoughton was tucked in bed upstairs. Down in the kitchen El and Cooley found used pots and pans stacked at one end of the table. A pile of dirty dishes sat nearby. A kettle of water was warming on the back of the stove.

Cooley fetched two large dishpans—one for washing, the other for rinsing—off their pegs on the wall. "Come on, El. Get the kettle and put some hot water in these." He banged the dishpans down on the table. "Share and share alike."

El felt himself grow angry. He was tired of Cooley's bossy ways. But with Mother sick, now was not the time for fighting. To forget his anger, he concentrated on getting each pan and dish scrubbed extra clean. This helped, he decided.

As they finished, Cooley offered to check the pantry, just to make sure they hadn't missed something that needed washing. A few minutes later he was back in the kitchen. "Hey, El, look at this!" He held up a large pitcher, partly filled with a thick batter. In the other hand he had a small jar.

"Mother must have been fixing us a special treat." Cooley held the pitcher so El could see inside.

"Looks like batter for buckwheat pancakes."

"Mother must have forgotten she started them. This jar was next to the pitcher, but I don't know what's in it."

El took the jar from Cooley. "That's easy. It's yeast—it's what makes the pancakes light and fluffy. You mix it in, leave the batter overnight, and it rises and gets bigger."

"I suppose you read all about it in some book," said Cooley sarcastically.

"No." El scowled at Cooley. "Mother told me. She showed me how to cook pancakes, too."

Suddenly Cooley's eyes brightened. "I have an idea! Why don't we cook the pancakes ourselves for breakfast? We can surprise Mother."

El had to admit it sounded like a good idea. What could possibly go wrong? "All right, Cooley," he said. "But I don't know if Mother added the yeast to this batter. She mixes it in the last thing."

Cooley looked thoughtful. "Well, the yeast jar was still sitting by the pitcher. And Mother's fussy about putting things away once they're used. I'll guess she didn't put it in yet."

El thought he should ask Mother, just to make sure. But he would have to wake her to do this. Besides it would spoil the surprise. He decided to take a chance. Even if she had added some yeast, a little more wouldn't hurt, he figured. It would just make them extra light and fluffy.

He took a wooden spoon and scraped a generous helping of yeast out of the jar. Then he stirred it into the batter and set the pitcher on the back of the stove.

To make sure the stove stayed warm most of the night, Cooley added another piece of wood to its low-burning fire. "There. Won't Mother be surprised! And wait until Father hears how well we managed."

The next morning El and Cooley got up extra early to start breakfast. They were careful not to make any noise that would wake Stoughton or Mother.

Eagerly El opened the door to the kitchen. Then both boys stared in disbelief.

The top of the stove was covered with a grayish oozing mass. It had gushed out of the mouth of the pitcher, spread over the top of the stove, and spilled to the floor.

"What a mess!" El cried.

"What happened?" Cooley wailed.

"I—I guess we put too much yeast in," El answered.

"What do you mean 'we'? *You* put the yeast in."

That Cooley! El thought. He turned and looked squarely at his brother. "Now, look here, Cooley, this was your idea, too. If Mother sees this mess and Father hears about it, we're both in for it. Remember, share and share alike!"

Cooley looked at the stove. Then he gave his brother a silly grin. "You're right, El. I wanted to do something really big for Mother, too."

El grinned back. "We surely did do something big for Mother!" he said, and together they burst out laughing.

Half an hour later, after much scraping and scrubbing, the stove was spotless. The floor had been wiped up and all the buckwheat pancake batter dumped in the woods.

El and Cooley decided not to say anything about the surprise breakfast they had planned. Instead, El put a kettle of water on to boil to make tea for Mother. Cooley fetched a pot of honey, butter, and a loaf of bread from the pantry. And he put a bowl of newly picked apples on the table.

By the time Stoughton came downstairs, breakfast was ready. But before El and Cooley ate, they took Mother some tea and buttered bread.

El was pleased to see how much better she looked this morning. And he noticed a look of relief on Cooley's face, too.

Mother nodded her head in approval as she tasted her tea. "And did you get all the dishes washed last night?"

El and Cooley bobbed their heads up and down.

"I must tell your father how well you've managed," she added.

El was relieved that Mother had forgotten to ask about the pancake batter. He did not dare look at Cooley. He could see his brother was trying hard not to laugh, and he was having the same trouble.

TEN

Townfolk and Countryfolk

El dodged his way through the early-comers to the fair. Father had sent him to the livestock area to run errands for the judges. The livestock judging was to take place this morning.

The Marion County Fair had opened yesterday in Indianapolis. The late October day was sunny and mild, good weather for a gathering. Farmers and their families had come from all over Marion County. By ten o'clock in the morning, the grounds around the county courthouse were filled with men, women, and children—farmers and townfolk.

Anyone who was a member of the Marion County Agricultural Society could enter the competitions. A lot of folks joined so they would have a chance to win some prize money. Father, who loved farming, was treasurer of the society and had promised that the prizes would be paid in gold coins. The farmers thought this was a fine idea.

Splashes of color from the exhibits made the grounds look festive. Rounds of cheeses were neatly arranged on one table, while crocks of butter sat on another. Samples of blue twilled cloth were draped side by side over fence rails. Rolls of flannels in rich tones of red browns and tans were shown together, while hand-loomed rugs were spread out a few feet away. Folds of fine white linen were displayed near the many-colored hand-knitted woolen socks.

Yesterday afternoon the judges had made their choices for first and second prizes in each display. Mother had won first for her butter, which made El feel very proud. The awards would be given out today, following the livestock judging.

Father spent his time making sure everything ran smoothly. Since this was the first fair in the county—maybe in the state—Father was anxious that it be a success. He believed that someday Indiana would be noted for its many farms. Already there were thirteen hundred farms in Marion County.

As El reached the judging area, he saw two boys ahead driving some hogs onto the grounds. Nearby the farmers had gathered with their livestock. There were horses, a few colts, mules, cattle, calves, oxen, and sheep. A large pen had been put in place for the cattle and another for the sheep. The oxen grazed quietly at the edge of the field. The horses and mules were tied to wagons or else were on leads held by a man or boy. Several men were finishing work on a pen of log rails for the hogs.

There was a lot of coming and going and hurrying about. The sounds of shouted greetings and orders mixed with the bleating of the sheep or an occasional mooed complaint from a cow.

Suddenly El heard the hogs squealing. Then he heard some angry shouts.

He ran toward the commotion. As he drew near he heard one farmer say, "John Johnson's boy seems to be having a mite of trouble with them fancy hogs

"Looks to me like Ollie's got more trouble than that," another farmer said with a laugh.

El worked his way through the crowd to the hogpen. Just as the men put the last rail in place, both Ollie Johnson and a bigger boy started for the pen's opening. All El could see was a mass of hog backs bobbing along, heading at a trot for the pen. Not far away more farmers were driving their hogs onto the grounds.

"I got here first," shouted the bigger boy. "Get your funny-looking critters out of my way."

"Quit your shoving, Jess Stiles," Ollie shouted back.

It looked to El as if there was a fight brewing on the grounds. Father and the judges wouldn't take kindly to that. One farmer had already gone home angry because the hogpen hadn't been ready when he arrived early this morning. It wouldn't do to have other competitors leave.

"I'll give you a hand," El called out. Moving quickly along the outer edges of the tightly packed bunch of hogs, he helped drive both boys' animals into the pen. One of Jess's hogs got to the opening, then suddenly veered off into the crowd. Leaving the others, Jess chased after it.

El and Ollie laughed as Jess disappeared.

"What's your name?" Ollie asked, once the hogs were all safely inside.

"Elijah Fletcher—El."

"My name's Ollie Johnson. Much obliged for your help. Pap will be along soon to give me a hand when the judging begins. Maybe you and I can take a look around after that."

El thought that sounded like fun. "See you later, Ollie." With a wave of his hand, he went on his way. He figured Jess could round up one hog by himself.

El hurried back to the livestock-judging area. Soon the judging began. He made sure all the competitors for each class were there on time. At last it came time for the hogs to be judged. One group of five hogs would win first prize, another group would get second.

The judges looked Jess's five hogs over carefully. Like the two groups of hogs that followed, they were razorbacks. Almost wild, these hogs were allowed to roam loose in the woods. There they found plenty of nuts, or mast, to eat. In the fall they were fattened up, and then butchered.

When it was Ollie's turn he herded five of his father's hogs into the show circle. El could see that the Johnson animals were a special breed, white in color and heavier than the razorbacks.

"Johnson bought those hogs out of state," one bystander remarked.

Ollie seemed nervous as the judges looked over his father's animals. His pap waited nearby with the second batch of hogs. Then the judges took a look at these. It was plain to see that the Johnson hogs were the best-looking of all.

The judges went off to one side to talk and make up their minds about the winners. It didn't take them long. They came back and awarded John Johnson both first and second prizes—a prize for each group of hogs he had shown.

With a shout, El ran up to Ollie and clapped him on the back. "That's showing them, Ollie!"

Ollie turned red in the face, and his pap straightened up and looked very proud.

Just then El saw his father making his way through the crowd. He was heading toward El and the Johnsons.

"Congratulations, John," he said. "I envy you those hogs—fine-looking animals."

"Thanks, Calvin," Mr. Johnson said. "And thanks to your boy here for his help. Ollie told me El gave him a hand."

Father nodded, pleased. "He's been a help to me today, too. I'm proud of him."

Now it was El's turn to look embarrassed. Yet he was glowing inside at Father's praise.

By the time the awards were handed out around noon, El and Ollie had become good friends. Maybe the difference between townfolk and countryfolk was not so big after all, El figured.

A NOTE TO READERS

"I have witnessed a total wilderness converted into a flourishing city."
—FROM THE DIARY OF CALVIN FLETCHER

The forest that once covered most of Indiana is gone. Only a few small patches of it, carefully preserved, remain in the rural part of the state. The clearing in the forest where Indianapolis began is now a web of paved streets with high-rise buildings. The city has spread so that it now covers all of Marion County. Interstate highways surround it and run through it. Over a million people live in the city that, during El's boyhood in the 1830s, was home to about seventeen hundred people.

In his lifetime, El witnessed the beginnings of this great change. He saw clapboard houses take the place of log cabins, and two- and three-story brick buildings crowd the center of town, filling the open spaces where he once played. New roads—some, at first, only partly cleared trails—were cut through the woods. They linked farmers with the town, which was a promising market for livestock, grain, and vegetables. The Madison and Indianapolis railroad reached the city in 1847, when El was a young man. Within the next decade Indianapolis became an important center in a rail network.

Four more children were born to El's family after the close of this book: William, Stephen Keyes, Lucy, and Albert, who was born in 1846. The eleven Fletcher children all lived to adulthood, and each received the best education possible. El and several of his brothers attended college in a time when few people did so. And though it was commonly thought outside the Fletcher family that schooling was wasted on girls, Maria went back East to school and became a highly educated woman.

When El grew up, he became a preacher. Cooley also took up preaching, and he traveled as a missionary to foreign lands. Calvin helped manage his father's properties. Miles became a college professor and state superintendent of public instruction. Stoughton, like his father and his Uncle Stoughton, became a banker. Maria took an active role in the life of the city, alongside her lawyer/educator husband, Cyrus D. Hines. Ingram became a banker and a businessman. All the Fletcher children, except Cooley, eventually settled in or near Indianapolis.

El's mother died in 1854, when he was thirty years old. To honor her, he recorded his memories of her and of his childhood. Most of the stories in this book, *A Clearing in the Forest*, are taken from those remembrances.